Lindie Lou

Adventure Series

Up In Space

An Adventure at the Space Needle

by Jeanne Beillustrated by Kate Willows

PINA PUBLISHING 🍍 SEATTLE

MAR 19

PINA PUBLISHING 🍍 SEATTLE

Text copyright © 2016 by Jeanne Bender
Illustrations by Kate Willows © 2016 by J.A. Zehrer Group, LLC
Cover and book design by Susan Harring © 2016 by J.A. Zehrer Group, LLC

For information about special discounts for bulk purchases contact:
lindielou.com/contact-us.html
Manufactured in the United States of America
Library of Congress Cataloging-in-Publication Data Bender, Jeanne

Summary: When Lindie Lou and Max land in the Emerald City, a new adventure begins! Lindie Lou says goodbye to Max and wonders if she'll ever see him again. Her new owners introduce her to life on a lake and the sites of Seattle. Follow Lindie Lou through the city, where she meets new friends and learns life lessons along the way. The *Lindie Lou Adventure Series* continues, as she discovers Rachel the Pig, sees flying fish, orca whales, and the gum wall. But her biggest adventure awaits... when she goes UP IN SPACE.

ISBN: 978-1-943493-20-3 (hardcover)
ISBN: 978-1-943493-18-0 (softcover)
ISBN: 978-1-943493-19-7 (e-book)

[1. Pets–Fiction. 2. Travel–Fiction. 3. Dogs–Fiction. 4. Adventure Stories, Airplanes–Fiction. 5. Saint Louis (Mo.). 6. Seattle (WA)]

Here's what kids told
Jeanne Bender about Lindie Lou:

The pictures were REALLY good! My favorite picture is of Lindie Lou's new house.

—Bella, age 6

I liked all the adventures Lindie Lou went on. When I read the part about the song, I started singing along.

—Nick, age 9

The words were easy to read. The chapters were just right for me to read.

—Ashlyn, age 7

To my
-amazing editor and sister, Nancy Kiefer
-talented illustrator, Kate Willows
-creative designer, Susan Harring
-inspirational mentor, Jean Trousdale
-dedicated friend, Carlos Irvine

Your encouragement and dedication
to the Lindie Lou Adventure Series
make it possible to bring Lindie Lou
to children everywhere.

Lindie Lou®

You are so willing to learn, love, and please.
You make writing this book a pleasure and a breeze.
When I close my eyes, I see your fuzzy, sweet face
It makes it easy to write about you UP IN SPACE.

—*Jeanne Bender*

Contents

Chapter 1

WE'RE HERE

The airplane moved down a long runway. It was traveling at a very slow speed. Lindie Lou looked over at Max. He was looking out the window.

Lindie Lou and Max had just landed. They were in a big white bird. Max called it an airplane. They flew together from Saint Louis, where Lindie Lou was born. She met Max in the baggage area at the airport. They came to the Emerald City to meet their families.

Lindie Lou didn't know what her new family looked like. Her former owner, Sherry, from Saint Louis, said one of Lindie Lou's new owners was her sister, Kate.

Sherry's husband, Joe, had driven Lindie Lou to the airport.

"You're going to have a good life," he said before he left.

Lindie Lou missed Joe and Sherry but was excited about meeting her new family and seeing her

New home.

Max's owner was picking him up at the airport. He flew in earlier, on another airplane.

"We're in the Emerald City," barked Max.

"I can't wait to see the city and meet my new family," said Lindie Lou.

"You'll get to do both very soon," replied Max.

Lindie Lou looked out the window.

"I thought we were in the Emerald City. Emeralds are green. All I see are gray and white buildings. Even the sky is gray," said Lindie Lou.

"Just wait and see. The Emerald City is green all right," barked Max.

Lindie Lou heard a tractor drive up to the side of the airplane. A man in a blue and green uniform pushed the door open. He walked over to Max and Lindie Lou.

"Time for you to leave the plane," he said.

The man lifted Lindie Lou's and Max's carriers onto a conveyor belt. He ran down the stairs, then he lifted Lindie Lou's carrier onto a cart, pulled by his

tractor. He set Max's carrier next to hers.

"Guess what? You're going for another ride," said the man as he jumped into his tractor.

He drove the tractor past many buildings. When they stopped, they were in front of a large door.

Above the door was a sign.

Lindie Lou looked up at the sign. Then she looked at Max.

"I thought you said we were in the Emerald City?"

"We are," replied Max. "Seattle is the name of the city. The Emerald City is a nickname."

"Seattle," repeated Lindie Lou. "I like the way it sounds."

The large door slid open and they drove inside a building.

"Do you know where we're going?" asked Lindie Lou.

"Yes, we're going to a waiting room where our families will meet us," said Max.

"How long will we have to wait?"

Lindie Lou looked **worried**.

What if her new owners didn't come?

"You won't have to wait very long," said Max. "Don't worry."

The man in the blue and green uniform, lifted Lindie Lou's carrier off the tractor and set it on the floor.

Lindie Lou looked around. She was in a room with a lot of luggage.

Max's carrier was put on a conveyor belt.

"Good-bye," barked Max. "Enjoy your new home."

"Wait a minute," said Lindie Lou. "Will I ever see you again?" She was sad to see him go.

"If you ever go to the Pike Place Market, I'm usually somewhere near Rachel the Pig."

"Rachel the Pig?"

"Yes. Everyone knows who Rachel is."

Max barked one last goodbye before he and his carrier disappeared around the corner.

Pike Place Market, thought Lindie Lou, *and Rachel the Pig.*

I must **remember** *these two things if I ever want to see Max again.*

Chapter 2

MY NEW FAMILY

Lindie Lou watched people pick up their luggage. Some of them looked into her carrier, but none of them picked her up.

When the last piece of luggage was gone, Lindie Lou looked around. She was all alone. She decided to lay down next to

Coco was her friend. He was a stuffed monkey. She found him in the puppy playground when she lived in Saint Louis. She had brought him with her.

I hope my new family comes soon, thought Lindie Lou.

Max said they would come for her, and **she believed him.**

Finally, her carrier was put on the conveyor belt. Lindie Lou jumped up.

Here we go!

Her carrier passed through a sliding door into a room full of people.

I wonder which one is my new owner? she thought as she looked at everyone's faces.

A lady in a yellow shirt came out of the crowd and looked at the paper taped to the top of Lindie Lou's carrier. Lindie Lou looked up at her and wagged her tail.

This must be my new mommy! she thought. *She has a very friendly face.*

"Hello there, Lindie Lou," said the lady. "You are so cute."

The lady took Lindie Lou out of her carrier and gave her a soft hug. Lindie Lou licked her nose.

"You are even cuter than the picture Sherry sent, and you have such huge paws."

This IS my new mommy, thought Lindie Lou. *She is nice and friendly and she smells good, too.* Lindie Lou relaxed in her arms.

Her new mommy carried Lindie Lou out to a little green car. She opened the front door and put Lindie Lou in a doggie car seat. She tucked her blanket by her side. The carrier went in the back. Lindie Lou looked to see if Coco was lying inside the carrier. He was.

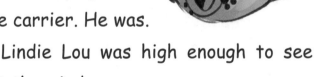

Lindie Lou was high enough to see out the window.

Her mommy talked into a speaker in the car.

"Hi Bryan, it's Kate."

Lindie Lou looked around. She didn't see anyone else in the car. *Who was her mommy talking to?*

"I have Lindie Lou and she is even cuter than I expected. Wait till you see her. She is so sweet and has the **biggest** paws I've ever seen."

"I can't wait to meet her," said Bryan. "Drive safely and I'll see you soon."

My new mommy's name is Kate, thought Lindie Lou, *and Bryan must be my new daddy. He's waiting for us? He must be at home.*

Lindie Lou looked outside.

I wonder where home is.

Kate was driving toward the Emerald City. Lindie Lou saw lots of yellow and orange trees. There were green trees, too, lots of them. Even the bridges had trees growing on top of them. She also saw green grass, green vines, and green bushes, peeking through the fall colors.

Now I know why this is called the Emerald City, thought Lindie Lou. *It is so GREEN. Max was right.*

Lindie Lou watched the city get

closer and closer. The buildings looked like giants. She looked up at the tallest ones. They were so high they touched the clouds.

Kate turned left and went down a long, winding road. The road led to a street with houses on the right side. There were rocks and green bushes on the left. Lindie Lou saw a beautiful blue lake behind the houses.

Kate stopped the car at the end of the street. She turned to Lindie Lou and smiled.

"Welcome home Lindie Lou," she said with a

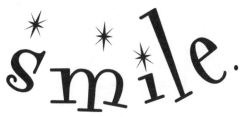

Chapter 3

MY NEW HOME

Lindie Lou saw a large white house. It had a colorful vine over the front door and a long green yard on the left. Behind the house was a bright blue lake.

I like it already, thought Lindie Lou.

Kate opened the car doors. She picked up Lindie Lou and her blanket in one hand, and the carrier in the other. She walked up the sidewalk and set Lindie Lou down so she could open the front door. Lindie Lou ran to the grass, paused, then turned and ran in the front door.

Bryan was in the kitchen. He came around the corner.

"There you are, Lindie Lou," he said. He bent down and scooped

her up.

"Isn't she precious?" asked Kate.

"She sure is," said Bryan. "I love her green eyes and you're right about these paws. They're huge."

Bryan put Lindie Lou down on the living room floor, so she could get to know her new home. Lindie Lou walked all over. She sniffed every bit of the room. In the corner she found a doggy bed.

"I bought that bed for you," said Kate.

Lindie Lou sniffed the room some more. Two stuffed animals were lying on the floor. One of them looked like a purple crab and the other looked like a pink lobster. There was a shiny yellow ball behind them.

"Those are your new toys," said Kate as she watched Lindie Lou's reaction.

Lindie Lou carefully picked up her new toys and put them in the doggy bed. Then she climbed in and curled up around them.

"She looks sleepy," said Bryan.

"She does," said Kate.

Bryan and Kate went into the kitchen. Lindie Lou heard them giggling.

I think they like me, thought Lindie Lou. *And I sure like them.*

Lindie Lou looked around her new home. It was light and full of soft furniture.

Wait a minute, she thought. *Where's my favorite blanket and Coco?*

Lindie Lou jumped out of her bed. She put her nose down and sniffed the floor. She ran around the room looking for them. The last time Lindie Lou saw Coco, he was in the carrier. She looked around the room.

I don't see the carrier anywhere.

Lindie Lou started to panic.

Coco was

missing!

Chapter 4

WHERE'S COCO?

Lindie Lou was very upset. She couldn't find Coco.

Coco was gone.

Kate peeked her head out of the kitchen.

"Are you enjoying your new home?" asked Kate. She was smiling.

Lindie Lou wasn't smiling because she couldn't find Coco. She looked behind the chairs, under the dining room table, and in the bathroom.

But no Coco!

Lindie Lou didn't give up. She sniffed up in the air and everywhere. She was frantic. She ran in a

pattern until she ended up in the kitchen. Her head was spinning so she sat down near Kate's feet.

Where's Coco? she thought. *I must find him. I promised to take care of him and now I've lost him.*

Lindie Lou took one more BIG SNIFF.

SHE SMELLED COCO!

He's here! thought Lindie Lou.

She looked around and spotted the carrier. It was in the laundry room. She ran over and looked inside. Her favorite blanket was there but

Coco wasn't!

I know he's here! I can smell him!
Lindie Lou sniffed some more. Her nose led her to a trash can in the corner of the kitchen.

Lindie Lou jumped up on the trash can but she couldn't reach the top. It was

too tall.

She scratched and scratched and
scratched!

Kate heard the noise from the other side of the room. She was sitting at the table drawing on her sketch pad.

"What do you want Lindie Lou?" she asked.

Lindie Lou kept **scratching**.

"Oh, I think I know what you want," said Kate. She walked over to the trash can, picked up Coco and brushed him off. "This must be very special to you."

Lindie Lou jumped up and tried to grab Coco out of Kate's hand. She missed and fell on the floor. Lindie Lou rolled over on her back and looked up at Kate.

"I didn't know this little monkey meant so much to you," said Kate. "Here, Lindie Lou."

Lindie Lou jumped to her feet and grabbed Coco. She carried him into the living room and over to her doggy bed.

She gently pushed the pink lobster and purple crab aside and put Coco in the middle.

"Meet your new friends," barked Lindie Lou. She climbed in with her stuffed toys and fell sound *asleep*.

Chapter 5

YOU CAN DO IT

The next day was Saturday. Kate and Bryan were sitting at the dining room table having lunch. Kate looked out the window.

"It's such a beautiful September day. Let's spend some time in the yard."

"I'm in," said Bryan.

Kate walked into the living room, opened the back door, and went outside.

Lindie Lou was lying in her doggy bed. She looked out the open door.

Something moved in the yard.

DUCKS!

She saw two ducks on the lawn. She climbed out of her bed and tiptoed through the back door. She crawled

very quietly, with her tummy low to the ground. When Lindie Lou got close, she jumped up and chased the ducks. They saw her just in time and flew up into the air. Lindie Lou ran after them, but they were too high. She tried but couldn't catch them.

The ducks landed on the lake. Lindie Lou kept running after them. Before she knew it, her paws were wet. She was standing in the lake, but she didn't know how to swim.

Lindie Lou looked to her left. Bryan was skipping stones on the lake. Kate was standing next to him, watching Lindie Lou.

If I could swim, I would catch them,

thought Lindie Lou. She stepped out of the water and shook her huge paws.

"Would you like to learn how to swim?" asked Kate. "The water is too cold for me, but not for you."

Kate went into the house and picked up Lindie Lou's shiny yellow ball. She threw it near the water. Lindie Lou ran  over and picked it up in her mouth. She brought it back to Kate.

"Good girl," said Kate. "You learn fast."

Kate threw the ball again. This time she threw it in shallow water. Lindie Lou ran after it. She carefully put one paw in the water, and then the other. Again she grabbed the ball in her mouth and brought it back to Kate.

"Let's do it again," said Kate. This time she threw it a little farther. Lindie Lou ran after it. When she tried to grab it, her face got wet. Lindie Lou stopped and shook her head. The water felt strange on her face.

"It's okay," called Kate. "You can do it."

Lindie Lou stuck her face in the water. She grabbed the ball and brought it to Kate.

"I knew you could do it," said Kate. "Now let's see if you'll get the rest of you wet."

Kate threw the ball even farther. Lindie Lou chased after it. She tried to grab the ball but missed. The ball

went farther into the lake. Lindie Lou
tried to reach it. Before she knew it,
her feet were off the ground.

She was swimming!

Lindie Lou kept going. She grabbed the
ball in her mouth, turned around, and
swam back to shore.

She gave the ball to Kate. Then she shook her entire body. Her ears flopped from side to side so fast, her head looked like a windmill.

"You can swim," said Kate. "I'm so proud of you."

I can swim? thought Lindie Lou.

Yes, I can swim!

Kate threw the ball a few more times. Each time Lindie Lou swam to get it. She loved to swim. She liked the way it felt to move her huge paws freely in the water.

The ducks were watching all the time. They were sitting on top of the water. They were too far for Lindie Lou to reach. She tried to swim to them but had to turn around because they were just too far away.

Lindie Lou watched Bryan walk over to Kate.

"Hey, good job Kate. Using a ball is a great way to teach Lindie Lou how to swim."

"And she learned so fast," said Kate.

Bryan and Kate threw the ball to Lindie Lou a few more times.

The sky above the backyard began to change. A dark cloud drifted over their heads.

"Looks like rain," said Bryan.

"Time to go in," said Kate.

Lindie Lou climbed out of the lake, shook the water off her fur, and followed them into the house.

Chapter 6

GO FOR A RIDE

Monday was a work day for Bryan. He liked to wake up to the morning sun. Today the sun's yellow rays reflected on the blue lake. Autumn colors framed his view from their bedroom window.

Bryan loved his job. He worked on computers. He made them faster and better. He worked downtown in a **tall** building. His office was on the twenty-second floor.

Kate worked from home. She set up an office in one of the spare bedrooms. She liked to draw on her computer. Her favorite thing to draw was animals. She worked for authors and gamers. She could see the backyard and the lake from her office. Kate worked four days a week. She worked longer days so she could have Mondays off.

Kate looked out the open window of the upstairs office. Lindie Lou was in the yard. She could go outside on her own. Bryan installed a new doggy door last Sunday. He also planted bushes and trees in the yard. They kept Lindie Lou from wandering off.   Lindie   Lou was lying in the sun, near the shore.

The ducks were back. They swam up to the yard and waddled onto the grass.

Lindie Lou stood up slowly. She was getting ready to chase them when Kate called out from the upstairs window.

"Hey Lindie Lou, do you want to

GO FOR A RIDE?"

Lindie Lou loved her ride from the airport. She ran across the yard, and through the doggy door. Then she rushed past the kitchen, slid on her tummy through the dining room, turned

right, and darted down the living room past the pink lobster and the purple crab.

I just slid across the floor, Lindie Lou thought. *It reminds me of the game I played with my brothers and sisters in the puppy playground. We called it the*

sliding game.

The thought made her smile.

When she reached the front door, she sat down and looked up at the doorknob.

This is the way out! thought Lindie Lou. She had seen Bryan leave the house many times from here.

"Looks like you're ready to go," said Kate as she rushed down the stairs.

Lindie Lou looked at Kate and then up at the doorknob.

Kate grabbed Lindie Lou's leash and hooked it to her collar. Then she opened the front door.

Lindie Lou followed Kate to the car. Kate lifted her into the doggy car seat.

I wonder where we're going, she thought.

They drove away from the house, up the long, winding road, and turned left onto a busy street.

Lindie Lou could see a lot of tall buildings in the distance. As they drove closer, the buildings got bigger. Lindie Lou jumped up and put her huge paws on the window.

She looked higher and higher as they drove past the tall buildings. They were so high she could barely see the tops.

"We're almost there," said Kate.

The car slowed down near a bright, colorful market.

A market, thought Lindie Lou. *Maybe this is Pike Place Market, where Max lives.*

Lindie Lou started jumping up and down in her car seat.

"What's all the fuss about?" asked Kate.

Lindie Lou turned toward Kate and

whimpered.

"I know you like to go for walks, but you're going to have to wait until I park the car."

Lindie Lou felt Kate pat her on the head. She had to wait, but she didn't want to. She wanted to go look for Max.

Chapter 7

SOMETHING STRANGE

Kate carried Lindie Lou to the entrance of the market.

Lindie Lou was looking for Max.

There were people selling flowers, jewelry, and fresh caught fish. T-shirts and artwork hung on the walls.

These colorful flowers are amazing, thought Lindie Lou. *They are even brighter than the autumn trees in Saint Louis.*

Lindie Lou and Kate made their way farther into the market. They could hear people shouting and cheering. As they came closer, Lindie Lou saw a man throwing something. He threw it over a table full of freshly caught fish.

"Here comes a salmon," yelled the man behind the table. Another man, on the other side, caught the big fish with both hands. Everyone clapped and cheered.

That was cool, thought Lindie Lou.

Out of the corner of her eye, Lindie Lou saw something strange. It looked like an animal, but it was big and it didn't move. Lindie Lou barked. Kate looked over to see what she was barking at.

"Oh, it's Rachel the Pig," said Kate.

Rachel? thought Lindie Lou. She remembered what Max had said in the airport before he left...

"Look for me in the market near
Rachel the Pig."

The pig was three times bigger than a real pig. It was made of metal and stood near the entrance to Pike Place Market. People were putting coins in a slot on its back. It was a giant piggy bank.

"Rachel the Pig," yelled a little girl as she ran up to it. The little girl's mom sat her on Rachel's back.

"It's your turn," said Kate. She lifted Lindie Lou up, unhooked her leash, and took her picture.

Lindie Lou liked to have her picture taken.

When Kate was done, Lindie Lou looked around the market. From the top of Rachel, Lindie Lou could **see** all over the market.

Max must be here somewhere, she thought. *He said he'd be near Rachel.*

Way in the back of the market, Lindie Lou saw something move. It was gray and white.

Could it be Max?

Kate lifted Lindie Lou off Rachel's back and set her on the ground. She put her leash on and walked to the right. Lindie Lou pulled Kate in the other direction, toward the gray and white object.

"Max?" barked Lindie Lou.

The object kept moving.

"Max?" barked Lindie Lou again.

The object didn't stop. It continued moving under the tables. Lindie Lou got closer. She could see it was a dog.

Kate tried to turn Lindie Lou around, but Lindie Lou kept pulling on her leash.

"Okay," said Kate. "Let's see what you're after."

Lindie Lou let out a **big loud bark.**

"MAX, IT'S ME...LINDIE LOU."

The object stopped, turned its head, and looked at her.

It was

Max!

Chapter 8

FOLLOW ME

Max ran over to Lindie Lou. She jumped up and tried to lick his nose.

"Hey little one, you found me." They chased each other in a circle. Then Max looked up at Kate. "I see you've found your new mom," he barked. "Do you think she'll let you come with me?"

Lindie Lou wagged her tail.

"This dog seems to be your friend," said Kate.

Lindie Lou looked up at Kate. She panted, tipped her head and looked into Kate's eyes.

"Follow me," barked Max.

Lindie Lou turned toward Max and pulled on her leash.

"Let's see where he's going," said Kate. They followed Max between the shoppers until he stopped at a fish stand.

"Hi, Max," said a man behind the

counter. "I see you brought some friends with you."

The man looked over at Lindie Lou and Kate.

"My name is Harry. It's nice to meet you."

"Hi Harry. I'm Kate and this is Lindie Lou."

Harry came out from behind the counter, wiping his hands on his apron. He was a strong, hardworking man, wearing a white t-shirt and a pair of blue jeans. He squatted down and looked at Max.

"Hi, boy. It's been awhile. I bet you came here for some smoked fish."

Max barked once and then turned around and walked toward the market.

"Where are you going?" asked Lindie Lou. "Don't you want some fish? I do."

"Later," said Max. "First, I'd like to show you around."

"But I'm hungry," said Lindie Lou.

"There's a lot of food in the market," said Max. "Follow me."

Lindie Lou tried to follow Max, but she was still on her leash.

"Looks like Max wants to show your puppy around Pike Place Market," said Harry.

"Is it safe to let her off the leash?" asked Kate. She looked around. They were far away from all the cars and inside a building full of people.

"It sure is," said Harry. "Max knows his way around even if they go outside. He's been hanging around here for a long time."

"Okay," said Kate. "Plus Lindie Lou has a tracking chip. It allows me to follow her, so I'm okay letting her go."

Kate knelt down and unhooked Lindie Lou's leash.

"Stay close to Max," said Kate. She watched them walk away.

Lindie Lou felt free without her leash on.

"This way," said Max.

They disappeared in the crowd of people.

"I have someone else I'd like you to meet," said Max.

He led Lindie Lou out one of the doors and onto the sidewalk.

Lindie Lou stopped.

"I'm not sure I'm supposed to go out here," said Lindie Lou.

"Don't worry. I won't let anything happen to you." Max sat down and looked at Lindie Lou.

Lindie Lou reached over and put her **huge** paw on Max's leg.

"Just stay close to me," said Max.

"I will," said Lindie Lou.

Chapter 9

THE MARKET

Lindie Lou followed Max across the street and up a wooden staircase. Max sat down at the entrance to a restaurant.

"Do you remember me telling you about the lady who works here?"

"Yes, you said her name was Dee..."

"Delight," barked Max. "Her name is Delight."

Delight heard them barking and came to the door of Lattie's restaurant.

"Hi Max, I see you brought a friend."

Delight bent down and picked up Lindie Lou. She took a closer look at her.

"She sure is a cute little thing," said Delight. "Would you like a bone?"

Lindie Lou panted with her tongue out. Max stood up and wagged his tail.

Delight put Lindie Lou down, went into the restaurant, and came out with two bones: a **big** one and a little one.

"It's nice to see you, Max. You've been gone for a while." Delight reached down and scratched Max behind the ears. Max looked up at her with happy eyes.

"Here you go," said Delight.

Max and Lindie Lou gently took the bones and walked back down the stairs.

Lindie Lou followed Max to a quiet spot near a fruit stand. They laid in the shade and chewed on their bones.

"You have a very good life," said Lindie Lou.

"I do," replied Max. "My owner lets me run free in the market during the day. I've made lots of friends here." Max looked over at Lindie Lou. "Is your life good too?"

"Yes," said Lindie Lou. "Coco and I like Seattle, and I have two new friends: a pink lobster and a purple crab.

We live near a lake. Ducks come to visit us in the backyard. I like to chase them. I even learned how to swim."

"Nice," replied Max.

Lindie Lou and Max chewed on their bones until they were done. Then Max stood up.

"Come on, there's more I'd like to show you."

Chapter 10

THAT'S DISGUSTING

Lindie Lou followed Max down a narrow road. It led to an alley under the market. They turned a corner and Lindie Lou froze. What she saw made her gasp.

"That's disgusting!"

she yelped.

"It's the

Gum Wall,"

barked Max.

The wall, in the alley, was covered from top to bottom with colorful gooey gum. Some of the pieces were pushed into the wall in round circles. Some hung like string. One piece looked like a big pink heart. It was made from blobs of

goopy, sticky

bubble gum. Some of the pieces of gum
spelled words like *I LOVE GUM* and
I AM HERE.

"Look at all the colors," said Max.

"Okay, but **yuck,**" said Lindie Lou.

She looked up at the wall. Some of the blobs of gum were pink, green, yellow, and orange.

"It's a little creepy but kind of cool," said Lindie Lou.

They watched a girl take a piece of blue gum out of her mouth and stick it on the wall.

"GROSS,"

yelped Lindie Lou.

Lindie Lou turned to run away from the wall, but she tripped on a crack, and fell toward the wall. One of her huge front paws got stuck in the gum.

"Ick!" squealed Lindie Lou.

She pulled her paw away from the wall. The gum snapped back into place.

"Eww," squeaked Lindie Lou.

"That's enough of that," said Max.

Lindie Lou followed Max back toward the market.

They turned a corner and climbed up a wooden ramp. At the top of the ramp was a place to sit. In front of them was a huge blue body of water.

"This lake is much bigger than the one near my house," said Lindie Lou.

"It's not a lake," said Max. "It's called Puget Sound."

"Puget what?"

"Puget Sound," repeated Max. "A Sound is a waterway that leads to the ocean. This one has many boats on it. Some are called ferries. The one in front of us is full of people and lots of cars."

"Where are they going?" asked Lindie Lou.

"The ferries travel to nearby islands. One is called Bainbridge, another Bremerton, and behind us is Vashon Island."

"I'd like to ride on a ferry someday," replied Lindie Lou.

Just then a giant fish jumped out of the water. Two more jumped right

behind it. They made a

HUGE SPLASH.

"Those are the biggest fish I've ever seen," said Lindie Lou.

"They're not fish; they're mammals," said Max. "They are called orca whales and are actually giant dolphins."

"They look like they're playing," said Lindie Lou.

"They are playing," replied Max.

Lindie Lou and Max watched the orcas jump and spin like dancers in a ballet. Then they all disappeared, one by one, below the surface of the water.

"Time to go," said Max.

"That was amazing," said Lindie Lou.

Max led Lindie Lou up a ramp, down the street, and around a corner.

"We're heading back to the market," said Lindie Lou. "You sure know your way around."

"Would you like some smoked fish?"

"I sure would," replied Lindie Lou.

Chapter 11

LESSONS

"Lindie Lou, can you find the way back to Harry's fish stand?" asked Max.

"I think so."

Lindie Lou could smell smoked fish.

The smell was coming from an open door in the market.

Lindie Lou led Max through the door. She stopped in front of a table.

"Here's the smoked fish," said Lindie Lou. She jumped up and put her huge paws on a wooden table.

"Get away from there," yelled an angry man. "Those fish aren't for you!" Lindie Lou jumped down and ran over to Max. She hid behind him. Max shook his head, stood up, and walked away from the fish stand.

"We're at the wrong fish stand," said Max. "I think you better follow me."

"That man scared me," said Lindie Lou.

Max looked at Lindie Lou.

"You've just learned two new lessons."

"First, don't expect everyone to be your friend. It takes time to earn someone's trust.

Second, don't think you know everything. It can get you into a lot of trouble."

"Okay and thank you," said Lindie Lou shyly.

Lindie Lou was glad she had Max for a friend. He was wise and very caring.

"I honestly can't remember how to get back to Harry's," said Lindie Lou.

"Okay. Come with me," replied Max.

"This place is huge," barked Lindie Lou.

Max led Lindie Lou to another building. Lindie Lou ran to the entrance and looked inside. "I see Harry's fish stand. It's over there."

Kate was standing in the hallway. She was looking for Lindie Lou.

"There you are!" called Kate. She was holding a bag of food and a bunch of flowers.

Lindie Lou **ran** up to her.

Kate set down her shopping bags and picked up Lindie Lou.

"I missed you," she said.

Max walked over to the smoked fish table and sat down. Lindie Lou wiggled out of Kate's arms and went over to Max.

"You will get more fish if you sit down," said Max.

Lindie Lou sat down.

"Here you are," said Harry. He took a piece of smoked salmon and tossed it to Max. Max caught it in the air. Then

Harry threw another piece to Lindie Lou. She caught it too.

"Good catch," said Harry.

"Let's eat it over here," said Max. He led Lindie Lou under a table near the back of Harry's fish shop.

Lindie Lou liked the taste of smoked fish.

It was kind of sweet, kind of fishy, and kind of smoky. When they were finished, Harry walked over and gave them each another piece.

Lindie Lou decided she **LOVED** the taste of smoked fish. When she was finished, she licked her mouth.

"I think you've had enough," said Kate. She reached under the table and picked up Lindie Lou. "It was nice meeting you Harry. And thanks for the fish." Kate held up one of her food bags.

"The ice, in your bag, will keep it fresh until you get home," said Harry. "Come again soon."

Kate nodded at Harry and then looked under the table at Max.

"It was nice meeting you, too."

Max licked his mouth.

Lindie Lou looked over at Max.

"I'll come back, I promise."

"I'll be here," barked Max.

Kate put Lindie Lou down and attached her leash.

"Now it's my turn to show you something really cool," said Kate.

Chapter 12

A SPACESHIP

Lindie Lou followed Kate to the car. She opened the back door and put her shopping bags and flowers on the floor. Then she walked to the front and lifted Lindie Lou into her doggy car seat. They pulled away from the market and were on the

move again.

Lindie Lou loved Seattle but missed Saint Louis, too.

I wonder where all my brothers and sisters are, she thought. *I hope I see them again someday.*

Kate parked the car on Broad Street, one block away from a huge park. She opened Lindie Lou's car door and put Lindie Lou on her leash.

"There it is," said Kate. "The famous Space Needle."

Lindie Lou looked up at a **huge** tower in front of her.

Is it a spaceship? wondered Lindie Lou.

Kate picked up Lindie Lou and walked toward the tower. She followed a path into a beautiful green park.

"Look at the cute puppy," said a girl in a blue sweatshirt. "Can your puppy play with us?"

The girl pointed at a group of kids playing on the grass.

"Sure," said Kate. "She loves to play. Her name is Lindie Lou."

Kate let Lindie Lou off her leash, and she ran after the girl.

"I wanna hold her," said one of the boys. He scooped her up and spun her around.

"I wanna hold her, too," said another boy. He tried to pull Lindie Lou out of the other boy's hands. Lindie Lou pushed them away with her huge paws and jumped to the ground.

Let's see if they'll chase me, thought Lindie Lou. She turned and ran away.

Chapter 13

THE CHASE GAME

"Let's chase her," said one of the girls. They all cheered as they chased Lindie Lou down the long green lawn.

This is fun! thought Lindie Lou. She ran in a big ᴄircle. Then she stopped, turned around, and ran the other way. One of the boys jumped at Lindie Lou, but he missed and landed on his belly.

"Way to go," yelled a girl from the group.

They were getting very close so Lindie Lou ran under a bush. The kids

tried to grab her, but they couldn't reach her.

"Come out little puppy," said one of the girls. "We won't hurt you. We just want to play."

What fun, thought Lindie Lou. *I like this game.*

After a few minutes, Lindie Lou ran out from under the bush. One of the boys was standing right in front of her. Lindie Lou ran through his legs.

"There she goes!" yelled the boy.

The kids started chasing her again.

"The chase game,

the chase game,"

yelled the boy.

Lindie Lou ran toward the girls.

"Here she comes," said a girl with long brown hair. The girls

screamed

and ran away.

"Now I'm chasing them," barked Lindie Lou.

She chased the girls to the end of the grassy area. The girls all hugged one another and fell to the ground laughing.

"She's so cute," said a girl with blond hair wearing a pink dress. Lindie Lou went over and licked her face.

The boys ran over. One tried to pull Lindie Lou's tail. Lindie Lou jumped up and ran away again. She saw Kate sitting on a bench at the end of the lawn and ran to her. All the boys and girls followed.

"The chase game! The chase game!" sang a little boy. "I like the chase game."

Kate bent down and picked up Lindie Lou.

"You sure made those kids happy," said Kate.

"We really like your puppy," said one of the girls. "Thanks for letting her play with us."

"You're welcome," said Kate.

"Lindie Lou, you are cool!" said a boy.

That reminds me of the song Sherry sang, thought Kate.

She started to sing.

Lin-die Lou you are cool and your friends think you're a jewel.

La la la   La la la la la   La la la la   la

All the kids started to sing...

La la la   La la la la la   La la la la   la

LindieLou.com/song

Kate held up one of Lindie Lou's huge paws. She waved good-bye to all the kids.

"Bye-bye."

They waved, turned around, and ran away.

Kate carried Lindie Lou toward the Space Needle. She was humming the "Lindie Lou Song."

Hm hm hmm   Hm hm hm hm hmm   Hm hm hm hm   hmm

Lindie Lou looked up at the Space Needle.

Are we going up in that giant space ship? wondered Lindie Lou.

Are we going up in space?

Chapter 14

UP IN SPACE

Kate carried Lindie Lou through a door at the bottom of the Space Needle. She walked up to a counter and checked in.

"Follow the people on your left," said the lady behind the counter.

Families were walking in a line toward a gift shop. Inside were all kinds of amazing things to buy.

There were Space Needle T-shirts, tables full of cups, spoons and jewelry, and even little Space Needle statues.

Children were walking around looking at all the Space Needle toys and the stuffed animals. Lindie Lou wanted to play. She tried to wiggle out of Kate's arms, but Kate held on tight. She walked over and stood in line with some other people. They were standing in front of an elevator.

"Time to go up, Lindie Lou. We're going up in space," said Kate.

Up in space?

thought Lindie Lou. *I wonder how high we're going to go.*

The elevator doors slid open. Everyone walked into the elevator. When the doors closed, Lindie Lou looked out the window. She felt the room start to move. It was moving up into the sky.

Lindie Lou could see outside. The city was getting smaller, and they were moving higher and higher. Kate held Lindie Lou very close. Lindie Lou looked up at Kate. She was looking out the window. Lindie Lou looked out, too.

The elevator operator stood by one of the windows.

"Welcome to the Space Needle. This building was built for the 1962 World's Fair. It's six hundred and five feet tall. Imagine more than one hundred men, who are six feet tall, standing on top of each another. That's how high this tower is." He kept talking until the elevator stopped.

When the doors opened, Lindie Lou looked around.

Wow! We really are up in space, thought Lindie Lou. They were at the top of the Space Needle. She saw people standing outside looking at the city. Kate held Lindie Lou up to the windows so she could see.

Puget Sound looks much bigger from up here, thought Lindie Lou.

"Mount Rainier looks really close," said Kate.

Kate walked around the deck. They looked down at the beautiful city of Seattle.

"Look, Lindie Lou. There's the park you played in with all the kids. And over there is the Seattle Great Wheel."

Oh boy, that wheel looks like fun. I'd like to ride on it, thought Lindie Lou.

"Just think of how high up we are," said Kate.

Lindie Lou leaned over the railing. She looked down at the ground. It was so far away. Suddenly she felt as if she was falling. Lindie Lou started to panic. She stiffened up and slid out of Kate's arms. When she hit the floor, she turned and ran back toward the elevator.

"Lindie Lou wait!" called Kate.

The elevator doors were open. Lindie Lou ran in and as the doors closed, she squeezed between the people and hid behind their legs.

Kate ran to the doors, but they

closed before she could reach them. Kate quickly pushed the "down" button. But it was too late. The doors wouldn't open and...

Lindie Lou was

gone.

Chapter 15

LOST

When the elevator doors opened, Lindie Lou saw she wasn't at the top of the Space Needle anymore. She was back on the first floor in the gift shop.

Lindie Lou walked over and stood near a rack of T-shirts.

I'll wait here for my mom, she thought. *I can see the elevator doors from here.*

I wish my mom would hurry up, thought Lindie Lou. *I don't like being all alone.*

"Hey, little puppy, you're not allowed in the gift shop," said a lady who walked over and tried to pick her up. Lindie Lou jumped out of the way and ran farther into the gift shop. She wasn't looking where she was going and knocked over a rack of sunglasses.

"What's going on over there?" asked a man in a gray uniform. He saw the sunglasses lying on the floor. Lindie Lou was standing next to them.

"What have you done?"

Lindie Lou turned and ran away. The guard chased her across the gift shop.

I wish my mom was here, thought Lindie Lou.

"I'll catch you," yelled the security guard.

Lindie Lou ran around a table and toward the elevator doors. She kept

watching for her mom. But the doors didn't open.

Some children entered the gift shop. They were with their parents. They saw Lindie Lou and went over to her. Lindie Lou wanted to play, but the guard was still after her. He was sneaking up on her from behind a rack of clothes.

"I've got you now," said the guard as he reached for Lindie Lou. She jumped out of the way, ran, and hid next to a bunch of T-shirts.

The guard knelt down, pushed the shirts out of the way, and grabbed one of Lindie Lou's huge front paws.

Lindie Lou

SQUEALED.

She pulled her paw away from the guard, ran around a corner, and into a group of stuffed animals. She sat very still.

Maybe he'll think I'm one of them, thought Lindie Lou. She tried not to breathe.

The guard came around the corner.

"You're not going to outsmart me again," he said.

Lindie Lou sat very still, but she had to breathe, so she took a sip of air. Then she blinked.

"There you are!"

Lindie Lou jumped up and ran toward the exit. All the stuffed animals went flying in the air.

A lady, who worked in the gift shop, tried to block the door.

"You're not leaving," she said. "Not after the mess you've made."

"Where's my mom?" howled Lindie Lou.

She ran under a table covered with Space Needle statues and crawled into a corner.

She was shaking.

Chapter 16

WHERE'S MY MOM?

The guard bent down and put his hand under the table. He waved it back and forth, trying to reach Lindie Lou. But she was too far away.

Lindie Lou looked over at the elevator doors. She wondered where her mom was.

I wish Max was here, thought Lindie Lou. *He would know what to do.*

The guard stood up and walked away from the table.

"I'll just wait for her to come out," he told the lady who worked in the gift shop.

Lindie Lou watched the lady. She was picking up sunglasses.

I didn't mean to mess things up, thought Lindie Lou. She curled up in the corner.

A little while later she heard someone call her name.

"Lindie Lou, where are you?"

Lindie Lou lifted her head.

It was

KATE.

Lindie Lou ran out from under the table. The guard was standing near the counter. She ran right past him and toward Kate. Kate rushed out of the elevator. She saw Lindie Lou running toward her. Kate knelt down and caught

Lindie Lou in her arms. Then she stood up, swung her around, and they rubbed noses.

"Oh, Lindie Lou," said Kate. "I was so worried about you."

"Does that puppy belong to you?" asked the guard.

Kate looked at him. He had his hands on his hips and looked very serious.

"Yes," said Kate. "This is Lindie Lou. She jumped out of my arms at the top of the Space Needle and ran into the elevator. The doors closed before I could reach her."

The guard shook his finger at Kate.

"You better hang on to that little puppy," he said. "Look at the mess she made."

Kate looked around the gift shop. A lady was putting sunglasses back on the rack and stuffed animals were lying all over the floor.

"Did Lindie Lou do this?" asked Kate.

"She sure did," said the guard. "Then she hid under a table where I couldn't reach her. I knew she'd come out sooner or later."

"We're very sorry," said Kate. "May we help clean up?"

"Yes, that would be nice," said the security guard.

Lindie Lou picked up one of the stuffed blue bears in her mouth and carried it over to the lady who worked there.

"Thank you," she said.

Kate helped pick up the stuffed animals. When they were finished, she picked up Lindie Lou, held her up to her face, and looked her deep in the eyes.

"Lindie Lou, you are too young to be on your own. Please don't run away again."

I learned another *lesson* today, thought Lindie Lou.

I AM much too young to be on my own.

Kate carried Lindie Lou out of the Space Needle and over to the car.

On the way home, Lindie Lou thought about the day. *What a*

crazy, amazing day.

Most of it was fun, some of it was strange, and some of it was kind of scary.

Lindie Lou's eyes started to get heavy. She rested her head on the doggy car seat.

I just want to go home, she thought.

Chapter 17

HOME

Kate drove her car away from the city of Seattle. She drove down the long, winding road near their house. Then she turned and followed the road to the end of their street. She stopped the car in front of the house.

"Wake up, Lindie Lou. We're home."

HOME,

thought Lindie Lou. **We're home!**

Kate set Lindie Lou on the grass and went back to the car to pick up her shopping bags and flowers.

Lindie Lou ran to the front door.

"Can you sit?" asked Kate.

Lindie Lou sat down and looked up at the doorknob.

"Good girl," said Kate. She opened the door.

Lindie Lou ran over to Coco.

"I saw Max today," said Lindie Lou. "And I met a giant pig named Rachel. Then I got stuck in a Gum Wall." Lindie Lou made a face. "And the best part was when I went

up in space."

Lindie Lou jumped up in the air as if she were taking off. When she landed, she looked over at the pink lobster and the purple crab.

"Hmm, I should give you names," barked Lindie Lou. She thought for a minute. "I know. I'll call you Evy and Manny." Lindie Lou had heard Kate and Bryan talking about some friends of theirs with the same names.

Lindie Lou picked up the pink lobster and put it in the doggy bed. "You're Evy." She put the purple crab next to Evy, "and you're going to be Manny," she said.

Lindie Lou sat back and looked at her new friends. Then she put Coco in the doggy bed next to them.

"Come and eat," called Kate.

She put a pink dog bowl on the floor with food in it. Something was written on the bowl.

That's my name, thought Lindie Lou. *COOL.*

When Lindie Lou was finished with her food, she walked over and looked out of the back door. She watched the ducks waddle around the yard. They were quacking away. She wanted to play, but she was full of food and getting tired. She went over and climbed in the doggy bed with her three friends and fell fast asleep. She was happy to be

home.

Chapter 18

PACKING

A few weeks later, Lindie Lou heard her parents talking upstairs. She climbed up the steps and looked into their bedroom.

"Come over here," said Bryan. He picked up Lindie Lou and sat her on the bed.

Lindie Lou saw Kate putting sweaters and walking shoes into a big suitcase. Bryan threw in a heavy sweater and his walking shoes, too.

"Do you think this is okay for the harvest party?" asked Kate. She held up a brown, furry costume with huge paws. "Maybe Lindie Lou and I will win the prize this year."

"Hey, what a great idea," said Bryan. "Should I go as Lindie Lou's brother Jasper?"

"Sure," said Kate.

"I wonder what your cousin Ronda will be wearing," said Bryan.

Jasper

"She always comes up with amazing costumes," said Kate. "Remember last year? She came as their state bird."

"Yes, I remember," said Bryan. She was an American goldfinch. Her whole body was yellow except for her arms. They were giant black wings. She even had real feathers sewn into her costume."

"Yes," laughed Kate. "She sneaked up on people and poked them with her big orange beak."

Kate was laughing so hard that she fell on the bed next to Lindie Lou.

Lindie Lou

howled.

"It will be good to see Ronda. She's such a hoot," said Bryan. I hope she lets me ride on her combine again this year.

Combine? thought Lindie Lou. *I wonder what a combine is?*

"I've never been to an organic farm," said Kate. "Ronda said her friends Mark and Patty would be happy to show their farm to us."

"I hope we get a chance to go to the Raccoon River," said Bryan.

"I'd like to bike the Racoon River Valley Trail," said Kate.

She looked over at Lindie Lou.

"Hey, we need a costume for Lindie Lou, too," said Kate. "Let's pick something up after the airplane lands. There's a pet store near the airport. Maybe we can find a bumblebee costume for her."

"Great idea," replied Bryan. "I hope she doesn't try to sting Ronda!"

They both giggled.

We're going to the airport? thought Lindie Lou. *And we're going to a harvest party? I've never been to a harvest party. I wonder what it will be like and I wonder where Ronda lives?*

Lindie Lou stayed with her parents

while they packed and talked about their trip.

During the night, Lindie Lou was so excited she couldn't sleep. She told Coco, Evy, and Manny everything she knew so far. She thought about Cousin Ronda dressing up like the state bird and remembered Bryan and Kate saying something about the Raccoon River.

I wonder where we're going, she thought.

"I'd like to take you all with me," she whispered to Coco, Evy, and Manny.

In the morning, Bryan put Lindie Lou and her favorite blanket in a bright blue travel cart.

"She looks like one of the stuffed animals in the gift shop," smiled Kate.

Bryan rolled Lindie Lou out to the car and strapped her into the backseat.

Kate stacked their luggage next to Lindie Lou and then jumped in the front seat.

Woo-hoo. We're going on another adventure, thought Lindie Lou.

She looked out the window and smiled as Kate hummed the Lindie Lou Song...

Hm hm hmm   Hm hm hm hm hmm   Hm hm hm hm   hmm

Lindie Lou Song

Chorus 1
LA LA LA
LA LA LA LA LA
LA LA LA LA
LA LA LA

Verse 1
L-I-N-D-I-E
L-O-U spells
Lindie Lou

Chorus 2
LA LA LA
LA LA LA LA LA
LA LA LA
LA LA

Verse 2
Lindie Lou
You are cool
And your friends think
You're a jewel

Chorus 2
LA LA LA
LA LA LA LA LA
LA LA LA
LA LA

Verse 3
You are a
Very lucky girl
'Cuz you've been
All over the world

Chorus 2
LA LA LA
LA LA LA LA LA
LA LA LA
LA LA

Verse 4
I can't wait
To see
Where you
Take me

Chorus 2
LA LA LA
LA LA LA LA LA
LA LA LA
LA LA

(Pause)

Chorus 1
LA LA LA
LA LA LA LA LA
LA LA LA LA
LA LA LA

Verse 5
You are my
Little Lindie Lou
And I love you

Chorus 2
LA LA LA
LA LA LA LA LA
LA LA LA
LA LA

Go to lindielou.com to listen to the Lindie Lou song.

Fun Facts

- Rachel the piggy bank, in Pike Place Market, collects $6,000-$9,000 every year and receives money from all over the world.

- More people bike to work in Seattle than in any other city in the United States.

- Seattle was the first city in the United States to play a Beatles' song on the radio.

- Many U.S. cities get more rain annually than the city of Seattle, but Seattle has more gray days.

- The restaurant on top of the Space Needle is the country's first revolving eatery. SkyCity is 500 feet up the Space Needle and rotates 360 degrees every forty-five minutes.

- Seattle is part of a geological region known as the Pacific Ring of Fire.

- The Washington State Ferry System is the largest ferry service in the country, carrying eleven million vehicles annually.

QUICK QUIZ

1. Why is this city called *The Emerald City*?

2. What two things did Lindie Lou do at the lake?

3. In what month do Lindie Lou and Max come to Seattle?

4. Name two new friends Lindie Lou met in the market?

5. Where did Lindie Lou have her picture taken?

6. What animals swim in Puget Sound?

7. Where did Lindie Lou think the spaceship-like tower was taking her?

8. Which Lindie Lou adventure did you like best?

9. Where did Lindie Lou get lost?

10. What three lessons did Lindie Lou learn?

Answers:

(1) It is so green because of the evergreen trees. (2) Chased ducks, learned to swim (3) September (4) Harry, Delight (5) On Rachel the Pig (6) Whales (7) Up in space (8) Learning to swim, throwing fish, meeting Rachel, finding Max, the gum wall, top of the Space Needle, lost in the gift shop, packing. (9) In the gift shop. (10) Don't expect everyone to be your friend, don't think you know everything, and she's much too young to be on her own.

175

Seattle • Calendar

January

CHILDREN'S FILM FESTIVAL. This festival selects more than 130 children's films from all over the world. These films are screened to more than 10,000 people during the festival's tour of about twenty US cities. http://childrensfilmfestivalseattle.nwfilmforum.org/

February

CHINESE NEW YEAR. The Lunar New Year Celebration features lion and dragon dancing, martial arts, a costume contest, face painting, and more! www.cidbia.org/events

YO-YO CONTEST. Come and watch some amazing yo-yo moves at the Pacific Northwest Regional Yo-Yo Championship on the Armory's stage at the Seattle Center. http://northwestyoyo.com/

March

ST. PATRICK'S DAY PARADE. Enjoy Irish heritage with a St. Patrick's Day parade, including Irish music, dancers, bagpipers, and pirates! Drill teams, dancers, and bands will march away for one of Seattle's best parades! www.irishclub.org/parade.htm

EMERALD CITY COMICON. A convention celebrating comic books and their characters, pop culture icons, and games. Come and meet a mix of celebrity guests and artists! www.emeraldcitycomicon.com/

April

WORLD RHYTHM FESTIVAL. Come and enjoy more than one hundred drums, dance and drum workshops, along with performances at the Seattle Center. www.swps.org

May

MAY DAY. Celebrate May Day at the Woodland Park field with games, songs, and dancing around the Maypole. Bring a potluck dish and watch the May Day fire ritual. www.wallyhood.org/2014/05/may-day/

SEATTLE MARITIME FESTIVAL. This festival features free harbor tours, tugboat tours and races, wooden boat building for kids

and a chowder cook-off.
http://seattlepropellerclub.org/vigor_seattle_maritime_festival_2014

June

SEAFAIR PIRATES LANDING. Watch the pirates land on Alki Beach and enjoy live local bands, dancing, storytelling, inflatable rides, and a pirate costume contest.
www.seafair.com/AnEvent.aspx?ID=4&SecID=889

July

SEAFAIR TORCHLIGHT PARADE. Come and enjoy colorful floats, pirates, and drill teams. The parade will include giant balloons, horses, clowns, and more!
http://www.seafair.com/AnEvent.aspx?ID=8

August

BOEING SEAFAIR AIR SHOW. Watch the Boeing Seafair Airshow featuring the Blue Angels and the Patriots jet team while hydroplanes race on Lake Washington for the Albert Lee Cup.
www.seafair.com/

September

ITALIAN FESTIVAL. Celebrate *Festa Italiana* at the Seattle Center with Italian food, music, dancing, art, and kids' activities. Come see bands from the Pacific Northwest area and marionettes!
http://festaseattle.com/

October

ST. DEMETRIOS GREEK FESTIVAL. Enjoy Greek foods like lamb, gyros, baklava, and calamari while watching dancers performing in costume.
http://seattlegreekfestival.com/

November

MACY'S HOLIDAY PARADE AND STAR LIGHTING CEREMONY. Watch the 9:00 a.m. parade filled with marching bands, costumed characters, floats, and Santa. At 5:00 p.m. enjoy the lighting of the 161-foot star and watch the fireworks afterward.
www.seattle-downtown.com/events/#dec

December

WILD LIGHTS. Come and see 500,000 lights in animal shapes, watch night creatures and real reindeer, ride a carousel, and listen to carolers at the Woodland Park Zoo.
www.zoo.org/wildlights#.VBKKhMJdXaZ

SANTA AT SMITH TOWER. Come and see the view from the top floor observation deck, enjoy cocoa and treats in the Chinese room, and get your photo taken with Santa!
http://smithtower.com/

Lindie Lou with her Brothers and Sisters

LindieLou.com/BooksShop

Places to go with

pets

and

pet-friendly

hotels in

Seattle, Washington

Find links to dog parks, pet-friendly hotels, restaurants, and dog sitters on our website

lindielou.com/places-to-go

TEACHERS, LIBRARIANS, AND PARENTS

Enjoy the Lindie Lou Adventure Series

Lindie Lou Adventure Series books are written for kindergarten through third-grade readers.

Parents and Teachers: Children connect with the main character, an adorable puppy named Lindie Lou. She takes them on adventures and teaches them not to be afraid. As Lindie Lou gets in and out of trouble, the reader discovers many life lessons about people, places and things.

Each book includes hints about where Lindie Lou is going, a calendar of events, links for places to go and a quick quiz. Extra content encourages children to continue learning even when the book is finished. After reading Book 1, *Flying High*, the other books in the series can be read in any order. They are not dependent on one other.

The Lindie Lou website, lindielou.com, provides additional learning tools in a user-friendly and colorful environment. The website provides pictures, videos, illustrations, games, a song, lyrics, and more. The "Lindie Lou Song" can be heard on the song page of the website. Children enjoy this upbeat tune. The lyrics and score are also on the song page.

Videos of author Jeanne Bender show her introducing Lindie Lou to young readers. In one video, the author writes a chapter of the book and encourages young viewers to follow along and develop their writing skills.

Readers who are slow to start reading enjoy the books' large text, colorful illustrations, and creative graphics. As young readers improve their reading skills, the books in the Lindie Lou Adventure Series transform from a colorful read-aloud to an independent read. Readers who excel at a young age will enjoy the age-appropriate story line.

Librarians can introduce the Lindie Lou Adventure Series to their students and teachers. The book series follows guidelines recommended by the **Common Core Standards for English Language Arts.**

Students like to read the book in many formats. Audio and e-book versions are available on the website. Young students also enjoy seeing the book projected on a large screen. They can follow the words and watch the color illustrations. This helps bring the story to life. Many students like to pick their favorite characters.

The Lindie Lou Adventure Series is also a perfect read for English-as-a-second-language students. The vocabulary and descriptions are well written and easy to understand.

Collaboration among parents, teachers, and librarians guides young readers to the joy of reading. The amazing world of adventure is often first introduced to children through books.

The Lindie Lou Adventure Series is a literary tool. The books are ideal for parents and teachers to read aloud, engaging for independent readers, and are colorful early chapter books for library users.

Adventure Series

- *Book 1: FLYING HIGH*
  Flying on an Airplane for the Very First Time

- *Book 2: UP IN SPACE*
  An Adventure at the Space Needle

- *Book 3: HARVEST TIME*
  Celebration on an Organic Farm

Where would you like Lindie Lou to go next?

About the Author and Illustrator

JEANNE BENDER
Author

Jeanne travels often and loves to write children's books. Her puppy, La Petite Lindie Lou Peek-a-Boo, inspired her to write the Lindie Lou Adventure Series.

Bender studied with literary coaches in Seattle, Washington and Oxford University in the United Kingdom. Bender lives in Seattle in the summer and in San Diego in the winter with her cocker spaniel La Petite Lindie Lou. They travel all over the world together.

KATE WILLOWS
Illustrator

Kate loves drawing and coloring cute little things on her computer. She creates animals and cartoons for everyone to enjoy!

Willows graduated from Ohio State University with a degree in art and technology and a minor in design. Willows lives in Columbus, Ohio, with her two cats, Castiel and Cocoa. She enjoys playing video games and watching cartoons in her spare time.